THE DESTINY RING

TAHIR SHAH

ESMERALDA RIGLEA

THE DESTINY RING

TAHIR SHAH

ESMERALDA RIGLEA

MMXXIII

Secretum Mundi Publishing Ltd
124 City Road
London
EC1V 2NX
United Kingdom

www.secretum-mundi.com
info@secretum-mundi.com

First published by Secretum Mundi Publishing Ltd in
Daydreams of an Octopus & Other Stories, 2022
Published in this edition, 2023

THE DESTINY RING

Artwork drawn by Esmeralda Riglea

A CIP catalogue record for this title is available from the British Library.

ISBN 978-1-914960-93-2

VERSION 21112022

Visit the author's website:
Tahirshah.com

Mustapha Khan resided in a little wooden shack he had built with his own two hands on the edge of his village – a shack shaded by a sprawling mulberry tree.

His days were spent tending a field, peppered with rocks, that had been in his family for as long as anyone could remember.

And his nights were spent listening to his wife snoring so loudly that the bed, the floor, and even the walls trembled.

With the snoring so deafening, Mustapha Khan would climb up onto the flat roof, lie back on a mattress, and gaze up at the stars. Picking out the constellations as his grandfather had taught him to do, he would wonder…

…wonder how his life might have been different had he not married the woman he had, or followed the first path that had presented itself…

…a path leading to an existence as an impoverished farmer – a farmer with nothing to his name but a scrawny patch of third-rate maize, a lame donkey, and the most pitiful shack in the valley.

As the first call of the muezzin rang out over the rooftops, Mustapha Khan would get up and stretch. As soon as he was upright, his wife would jolt awake, and shift from snoring to barking.

Her lungs swelling with breath, she would
begin the morning's tirade – snarling
at her husband for being stupid,
careless, and good for nothing.

His ears long since deaf to the onslaught, Mustapha Khan would stroll down to the stream and wash in the cool, glinting water.

Once clean, he would pause on an old tree stump, stare at the patterns playing over the surface of the water, and thank Providence for his life.

It was true that a great many men possessed far more than he. But, as he considered it, there were many who had far, far less.

One evening at the onset of summer,
Mustapha Khan's cousin came to stay.
His name was Feroze, and he was a respected
map-maker in the court of the king.

The two of them had been brought up together, playing in meadows, splashing in streams, speculating about the adventures they would have.

After a dinner of roasted lamb and pilau, the two men went up onto the roof to reminisce. High above, the vast canopy of stars glinted and gleamed, and the full moon shone down, bathing them both in its ghostly light.

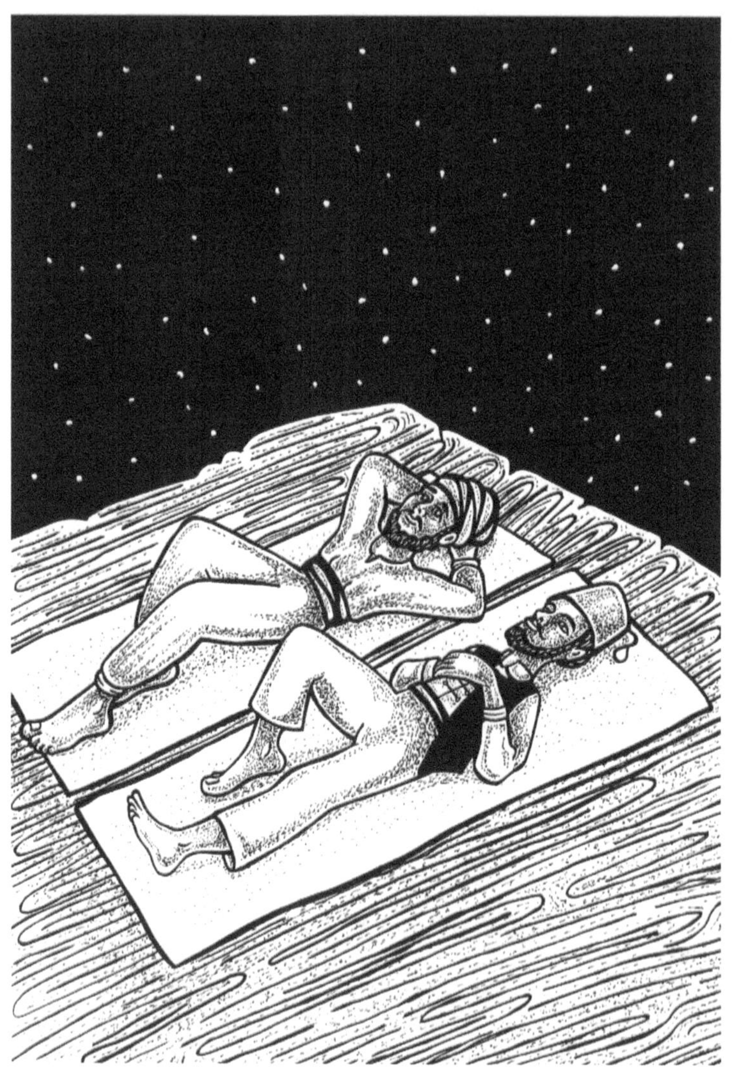

Lying side by side, staring up at the stars, it was as though they were boys together again, although Feroze was better dressed than his cousin, had more money in his pockets, and enjoyed a far more impressive career.

The farmer was about to declare satisfaction with his modest lot when his wife began snoring in the room below.

Staring up at the stars,
his expression tightened and he sighed.
'Where did I go wrong?' he whispered.

His cousin sat up and said:
'You chose a path that appeared to be the easy one – marrying the woman you did, and inheriting the field as you did, and…'

‘*And…*?’

‘And that path led to an adequate life,
but one that’s been lived a thousand,
thousand times before.’

Groaning at his stupidity,
Mustapha Khan sighed again.
'I'm a fool,' he said. 'A fool, for not setting out
on the road like you did – for not pitting
myself against whatever came my way.'

‘Now, now,’ Feroze riposted. ‘There’s no sense in having regrets.’

'Yes, there is… For unless you are deafer than deaf, you can hear the noise of that wretched woman down there. I get eight hours of snoring each night, and all hours of the day are filled with her infernal barking.'

The successful cousin leaned over and tapped Mustapha Khan on the shoulder. 'Listen to me,' he said.

‘What?’

‘It’s never too late to make a change.’

The farmer let out a snort.
'Of course it is,' he answered.
Feroze shook his head assuredly.
'No, no, no,' he replied. 'Believe me,
it's *never* too late for a new beginning.'

At the end of a week, the farmer hugged his cousin, and vowed to remember what he had been told up on the roof – that it was never too late to make a change.

And with that, the two men strolled to the end of the lane and hugged one last time.

Feroze was about to mount his stallion when something caused him to pause. ‘Sometimes in life,’ he said softly, ‘we don’t perceive opportunities when they come for us. It’s not that we’re blind to them, but that we’re not ready for them.’

The farmer wasn't quite sure of the point his cousin was trying to make, so he just smiled.

As he did so, Feroze said:
'The greatest secret in life is to have faith in one's destiny – and that means making choices we might not normally make.'

'You mean, like planting a new crop in the field?' asked the farmer.

‘Perhaps, yes, or even something more significant than that. You see, what’s important is to trust.’

‘To trust in what?’
‘To trust in your own honesty.’

Unsure what his cousin was going on about, Mustapha Khan wished he would stop trying to make the point he was making. Taking hold of the stirrup, he waited for Feroze to mount his horse.

But his cousin didn't ride away.

‘Last month, a trader arrived at the royal court with gold and perfumes from the Orient,’ Feroze said. ‘Having been rewarded, he was sent to me, so that I could make a map of the route he had taken.

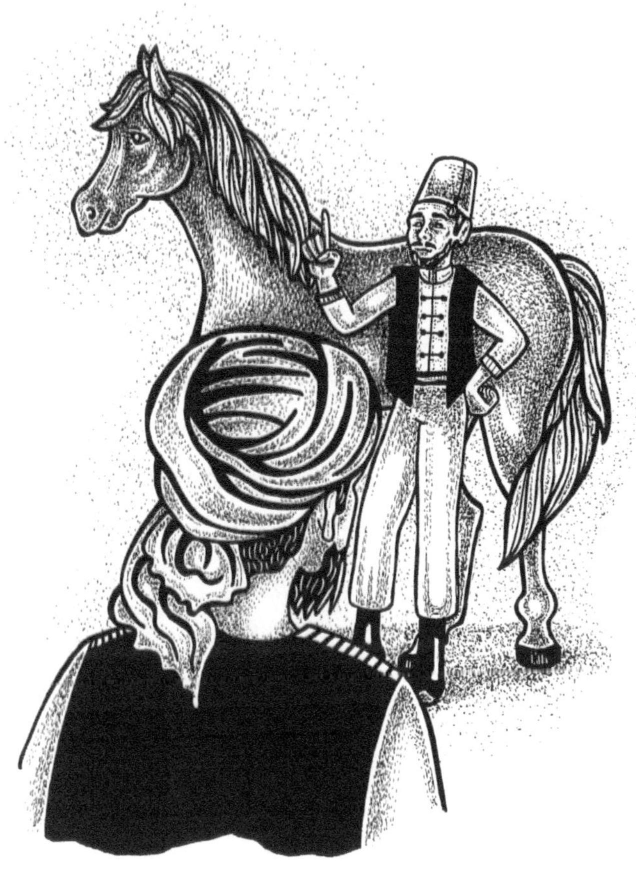

'We spoke about travel and adventure, and he described all manner of wondrous regions – with outlandish flora, exotic kingdoms, and warring tribes. I asked him for the strangest thing he had seen in all his travels.'

‘What was his reply?’
‘It was curious. You see, he didn’t say anything. Rather, he slipped a ring off his finger and presented it to me.’

Feroze twisted a ring off his
finger and gave it to his cousin.
'What is this?' asked Mustapha Khan.

His cousin looked the farmer
squarely in the eye.
'It is a destiny ring,' he said,
before turning his horse and setting off.

Mustapha Khan stood at the edge of the road and watched as the trail of dust billowed away towards the horizon.

When Feroze and his steed were well out of sight, the farmer glanced down at the ring. Made from the purest gold, it was adorned with an unusual geometric pattern.

But the thing that caught Mustapha Khan's attention wasn't the metal, or the interlaced motif – but that when he moved his hand, the ring rattled.

As the farmer tended his maize that day, his mind was on his cousin's visit, and on whether he ought to take the destiny ring to the bazaar and see what he could get for it.

The more he tried to put the precious gift out of his head, the more he thought about it. Making his way back to the shack at the end of the day, the farmer glanced down at his finger again.

Suddenly, he was overcome with angst. If his wife caught sight of the ring, she would ask a thousand questions, and order him to hand it over to her at double speed. So, just before he trudged inside the shack, Mustapha Khan twisted the destiny ring off his finger and stuffed it into his pocket.

All through dinner, his wife barked at him for not being half the man his cousin was – for owning a lame donkey instead of a stallion, and for having neither ambition nor dreams.

Early in their marriage, the farmer might have reacted, but far too much time had passed for Mustapha Khan to care.

When the meal was over,
he climbed up onto the roof, gazed up
at the kaleidoscope of constellations,
and lost himself in his imaginings.

As he stared up at the nocturnal
firmament, Mustapha Khan sensed
warmth in his loose cotton trousers,
as though something were burning.

Confused at what was happening, he thrust a hand into the pocket, his fingers closing around the ring – now mysteriously warm to the touch.

Holding the destiny ring up to the moonlight, the farmer heard it rattling, even louder than it had that morning.

With care, Mustapha Khan dug
a thumbnail beneath the bezel.
To his surprise, the top of the
ring flipped back on a hinge.

Something was sitting there in the cavity…
Something triangular and hard.
Tapping it onto his palm, the farmer
screwed up his eyes.

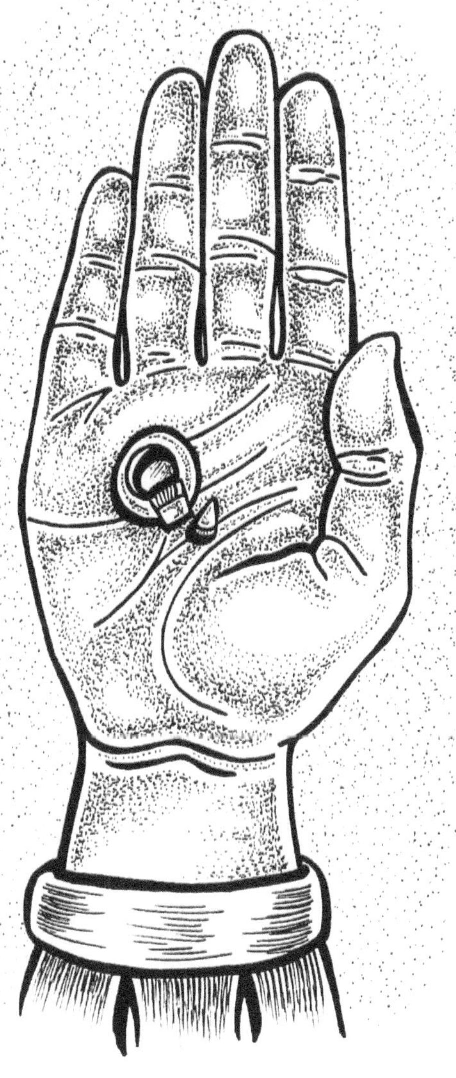

It was a seed, the likes of which
he had not encountered.

Mustapha Khan was well aware that people were known to wear so-called 'poison rings'. For centuries, unsuspecting foes had been knocked down with a few grains of arsenic when gorging themselves on a meal.

But however much he racked his brains,
the farmer couldn't remember ever hearing
of a hollowed-out ring which contained a seed.

That night, as his wife snored, Mustapha Khan hurried down to the garden. Having dampened the ground with a little water, he planted the seed.

Next morning, the farmer went out into the field and inspected the crop of maize. All the while, his mind was on the gold ring, and on how much he might get for it in the market. More than once he set off towards the town. But each time, he turned on his heel and traipsed home.

Tongues gossiped in the bazaar, none more than in the gold bazaar. An impoverished farmer turning up with such a precious-looking ring would raise suspicions. And with wagging tongues, it wouldn't be long before his wife would hear of the destiny ring.

By the evening, Mustapha Khan was worn out – from worrying about the ring and its value, rather than from toiling over the meagre crop of maize. As he approached the shack, the shadows lengthening, he heard the sound of laughter.

Inside, he found his wife and her sister
– both in high spirits.

'While you were wasting your time in the field,
I was finding treasure!' his wife hissed.
'*Treasure*?' the farmer echoed.
'A ring! A gold ring! I found it under
the pot in the bedroom.'

The farmer was about to explain that it was *his* property, a gift from his cousin, when his wife launched a tirade at him again.

‘I wonder where it came from?’ she said. ‘From the Almighty!’ her sister cried. ‘He is rewarding you with riches for putting up with that worthless husband for so long!’

The farmer's wife gloated.
Then, holding the ring to a candle's flame,
she cackled with greed and delight.

‘Yes, dearest sister, I believe you are right,’ she said. ‘It’s destiny from the Almighty for enduring the most awful man that ever lived.’

The farmer cleared his throat.
'What shall we do with it?' he asked.
'*WE*?' bawled his wife. 'There is no *we*... there is only *ME*. I'll go to the bazaar tomorrow morning and sell it. Then I shall spend the money on myself!'

As soon as daybreak brought colour to the valley, the farmer's wife hurried from the shack, paced to the market, and sold the ring. Being as rare and unusual as it was, she was given a fortune – a fortune she began to spend right away.

By nightfall, she arrived home with sixteen mules laden with kaftans, perfumes, and anything else that had caught her eye. The stall-keepers in the bazaar had never known a day of business like it.

Mustapha Khan stepped out to see the caravan of goods coming up the path, just in time to hear his wife yell at him: 'Don't think for a minute I got you anything, because I didn't!'

As the riches were borne ceremoniously into the shack, the farmer worried over what he would tell his dear cousin.

The thought of Feroze and the ring made him remember the curious seed – the one he had planted in the garden.

With his wife crooning over her kaftans inside, Mustapha Khan slipped out into the garden and peered at the ground.

He scratched his head.
No, no, no… that couldn't be right.

In the precise spot where he had buried the seed the day before, there stood a plant. No frail little shoot, or even a sapling, it was a fully grown tree.

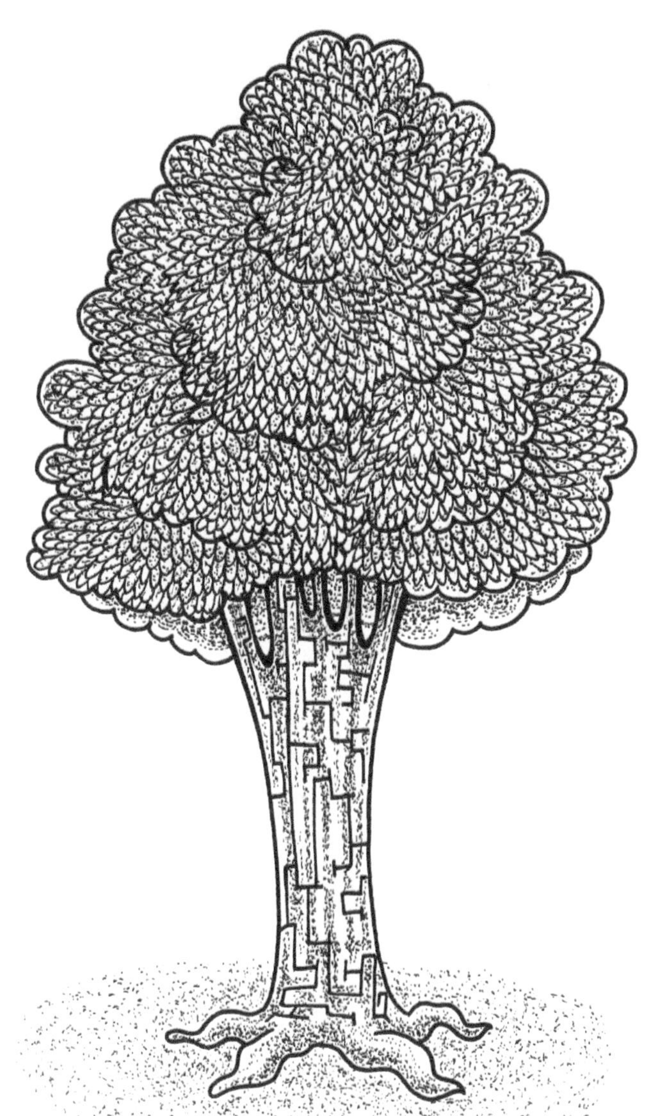

The farmer assumed someone was playing tricks on him, even though no one had seen him plant the seed.

Stepping up to the mottled trunk, he took one of the leaves in his hand and examined it. In a lifetime of farming, he had never seen a pattern like it.

The size of a man's hand, the leaf was covered in an interlaced zigzagging design, almost as though it were a map of a maze.

Taking another of the leaves at random, Mustapha Khan noticed it bore quite a different pattern… as did all the leaves. Stranger still was the fact that whenever his fingers brushed against one of the leaves, the pattern changed.

As he stood there, delighting in the way the leaves altered when he touched them, a little fruit on one of the branches began glowing a deep, unearthly red.

Peering at it, the farmer watched as the fruit seemed to swell in size, the colour deepening as though it were ripening before him.

Intrigued, Mustapha Khan reached out and picked the pod from the tree. The fruit darkened as it touched the farmer's fingers. Then, as he watched in astonishment, it seemed to peel itself.

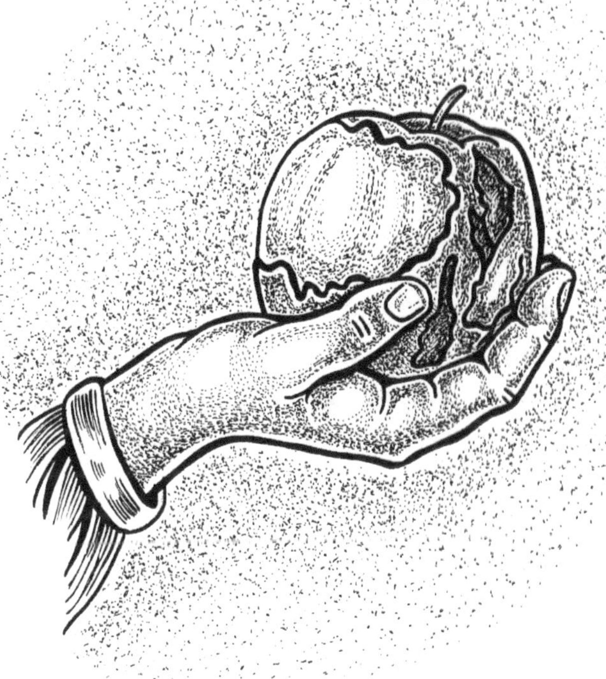

The outer layer fell away, revealing an emerald-green interior all glistening and scented. Without thinking, Mustapha Khan slipped the fruit into his mouth and began to chew.

Never in all his life had he experienced such consistency or taste. The fruit was both hard and soft, sweet and sour, and seemed to tingle against his tongue as though it were from another world.

As he chewed the emerald-green flesh, his mind filled with a stream of random memory:

Sitting on his uncle's lap.
A dog with three legs.
A mountain beyond the horizon.
Twelve scorpions in a bucket.
The late-summer moon.
A desert's dunes.

At that moment, Mustapha Khan felt something hard in his mouth. Assuming it to be the fruit's stone, he spat it onto his palm.

To his surprise, the stone wasn't actually a stone at all. Rather, it was what looked like an emerald-green eyeball, fashioned from crystal. Right away, the farmer wondered who would have wanted to play a trick like this on him.

He stood there in the garden for a minute or two, trying to make sense of the seed, the tree, the fruit, and the crystal eye.

All Mustapha Khan could conclude was that, having stolen the gold ring, his wife was now doing her best to make it seem as though her husband was a madman. It was a sure-fire way of taking away the lame donkey, the rocky field, and the shack, leaving him with nothing.

So, slipping the crystal eye into his pocket, he paced back through the garden to the shack, where his wife was adorned with satins and silks.

'Get out of here!' she bayed as soon as she saw him. 'My sister is coming over, and so are her friends!'

‘But where will I go?’
the farmer said dejectedly.
‘Go up to the roof, sleep on the mattress, and keep out of my way! Now that I have such fine possessions, I’m ashamed to be seen with you!’

So, Mustapha Khan climbed up to the roof and lay out under the stars. A great many men might have been incensed had their wife spent so much money on herself. But the farmer didn't care much for material possessions. He had never had much, but had never starved either.

The way he saw it, those with too much in life had worries that mirrored their wealth. Thanking Providence for everything he had been given, the farmer gazed out at the firmament and fell fast asleep.

When Mustapha Khan woke the next morning, dawn had already broken over the horizon, the shack and the fields around it bathed in golden-yellow light.

As he sat upright on the mattress, his hand slipped into his pocket, his fingers brushing against the eye. Frowning, he remembered the emerald-green fruit, and the strange crystal object it had contained.

Fishing it out, the farmer observed it in the morning light. Although emerald green in colour, the eye appeared to bear a pattern tattooed just beneath the surface.

As with the leaves of the tree on which the fruit had grown, the design was intricate and alluring.

Bewildered, Mustapha Khan couldn't understand how the seed had matured so swiftly, and how the tree it had become bore a fruit within which was a crystal eye.

As he pondered the events of the previous day, the farmer heard his wife cursing him downstairs.

Without thinking, he cursed her back:
'Oh, how I wish that damned
woman would vanish!'

Then, climbing down, the farmer
prepared himself for the morning's tirade.

But it did not come.

Mustapha Khan couldn't understand it…
his wife wasn't there. He searched the shack,
the garden, and the field, calling her name.
The bed in which she had been sleeping was
still warm, and all the expensive kaftans were
heaped up where she had left them.
There was no sign of her.

Breathing in deeply, the farmer strained to work out what had happened. All he could think of was that his wife had gone off to boast to the neighbours about her new clothes. So, he waited for her to come home and holler at him.

The day passed, and still his wife didn't return. As dusk approached, Mustapha Khan recalled how he had been holding the crystal eye when he cursed his wife.

Frowning, he climbed back up onto the roof, sat on the mattress, and looked hard at the eye. 'This makes no sense,' he whispered to himself. 'I'm certain she's playing a trick on me!'

With the eye still on his palm, the farmer caught a flash of his field. But instead of being all rocky as it was, he imagined it with the most magnificent crop of ripened maize.

As the image slipped onto the stage of his mind, the emerald-green eye seemed to blink. Gasping, he fell backwards, horrified at himself for having been fooled. But something was nagging at Mustapha Khan.

He climbed down from the roof, paced through the garden, and down to the field. There, shaded by the tall tree – the seed of which had been planted only hours before – was the most marvellous field of maize.

Agog, the farmer stared at the crop,
unable to think straight.
'What sorcery is this, that caused my
wife to vanish and the maize to thrive?!'
he cried.

All next day, as Mustapha Khan harvested the crop, his mind whirred away on the mysteries of the destiny ring.

By nightfall, the farmer's hands were sore and bleeding from toil. Even though his wife was the bane of his life, she usually prepared an evening meal. With her gone, and hungry from bringing in the harvest, Mustapha Khan fished the crystal eye from his pocket.

‘I wish I had a banquet fit for a king!’
he exclaimed with a chuckle.

No sooner had the words left his mouth than a feast of succulent dishes appeared, the likes of which the farmer had only ever imagined in his wildest dreams.

There were platters of kebabs and roasted chickens lying on fragrant beds of rice, tureens of spiced stew, silver salvers laden with exotic dishes from far-off lands, and great pails of rare fruits.

Mustapha Khan ate until he could eat no more.

He felt guilty at resorting to the higher power to serve his own needs. But, as he pondered it, his wife had lavished the money from the ring on clothing – while he had merely used the sorcery for something to eat.

Hardly having made a dent on the banquet, the farmer climbed up onto the roof and stared up at the stars. In a universe of mysteries, the night sky was the one certainty he could rely on.

Opening his fist, he peered at
the crystal eye and whispered:
'Oh, how I wish I could be transported
to a distant kingdom, and arrive there in
a caravan of wonder!'

The emerald-green eye seemed to blink, a sudden surge of energy knocking the farmer backwards onto the mattress. A moment later, there was no farmer, mattress, or rooftop.

Far away, the royal palanquin of a prince was approaching the capital of the Mughal emperor, Babur. His opulent caravan snaked its way through valleys and across plains towards Agra.

Stretched out mile after mile against the setting sun, it comprised outriders, legions of cavalry, and warriors striking giant timpani. All in all, there were six hundred camels, each of them laden with treasure – crates of gold coins, diamonds, and precious gems.

As the last vestiges of dusk melted into night, the great cortege reached the city.

In the light of a thousand burning torches,
the soldiers, attendants, camp followers,
and the vast treasure slipped through
the fortified gates of the citadel.

Having been transported in the blink
of a crystal eye from the rooftop of his
shack to the silken luxury of the palanquin,
the farmer pinched himself.
It was no dream.

Swallowing hard, Mustapha Khan wondered how on earth he had come to be dressed in the finery of a prince. As he wondered, he heard heralds sounding the imperial welcome from the battlements.

The next thing he knew, the farmer was being borne in the torchlight to the palace in which the emperor resided.

His stomach knotting in trepidation, his mouth bone dry and his brow beaded with perspiration, Mustapha Khan rehearsed what he would say by way of explanation.

He imagined himself pleading for his life
as an imperial executioner prepared to
swipe off his head.

But, to his amazement, there was no sense of hostility. Rather, the farmer was ushered into a private apartment, where he was offered refreshments from solid-gold vessels. When refreshed, he was received in the throne room by Emperor Babur himself.

Playing his part, Mustapha Khan clapped his hands, ordering his retainers to lavish his host with casks of rare perfume, sacks of gold coins, and mountains of precious gems.

Perched on his throne, the emperor surveyed the offerings with pleasure. Although no stranger to unimaginable wealth, he was astonished.

Once the gifts had been presented, Babur entertained his distinguished visitor with a sumptuous feast. As they dined, acrobats cavorted and storytellers regaled the court with tales of wonder.

The emperor could think of nothing except for learning the source of the visitor's wealth. Naturally, good manners prevented him from enquiring. So, as soon as the court had retired for the night, Babur dispatched his spies.

Next morning, the court vizier reported: 'Your Highness, it seems as though your guest is so prosperous that there's no end to his fortune.'

'What is the name of his kingdom?!'
cried the emperor.
'Alas, Your Magnificence, it is unknown.'

Emperor Babur's face flushed with ire. 'At least explain how such immense prosperity has been accumulated.'

Squirming, the vizier babbled apologies.
'It is not known Your Majesty,
Commander of Land, Sea, and Stars!'

Dissatisfied, the emperor ordered for the spies to be dispatched a second time, to get answers on pain of execution. That evening, the vizier reported once again…

'Your Imperial Highness,' he cooed unctuously, 'our informants have learned that the prince regards almost all material possessions with contempt.'

‘*Almost*?’ the emperor intoned.
The vizier took a step back so that he
might stoop all the lower in a bow.

'It appears, Your Magnificence, that there is but one object to which our distinguished visitor apportions any value at all.'

Babur pressed the tips of his fingers together in interest.

'What is it?' he spat.
The vizier squirmed.
'An eye, Your Majesty.'

‘An *eye*? What kind of eye?’

‘One fashioned from crystal. The prince keeps it upon his person both day and night.’

Lowering his mouth so as to be in line with the emperor's ear, the vizier whispered: 'Would His Excellency wish for the crystal eye to be acquired?'

Babur leaned back into the throne and,
narrowing his eyes, he gave voice
to his thoughts:

‘If our guest has indeed such incalculable wealth,’ he said, ‘it is likely he has a jinn at his service – more likely than not the jinn is trapped in the eye of which you speak.’

‘And so, Your Magnificence,’ the vizier
crooned, ‘what ought to be done?’
Again, the emperor leaned back as he thought.

After a long pause, he replied:
'There would be no good in simply relieving
him of the eye. After all, the jinn may have
been given instructions to reduce my kingdom
into dust. Instead, send for the prince to
appear before me.'

Within the hour, dressed in his finest costume, Mustapha Khan was standing before the emperor's throne.

Welcoming his guest with the respect reserved for a visiting monarch, Babur invited him to sit. Sweetmeats and sherbet were brought. Then, beckoning the vizier close, the emperor instructed him to send the courtiers away.

Once they were alone, Babur smiled
from the corner of his mouth.
'I must say that I am intrigued,'
he said, selecting his words with care.

The farmer swallowed hard.

'*Intrigued*?'

'Indeed. You see, I wonder how a prince such as yourself has been blessed with such fortune.'

Mustapha Khan glanced down at the floor.
'Nothing is quite what it seems, Your Majesty.'
Babur leaned forwards.
'How so?' he whispered.

Mustapha Khan explained everything that had happened since his favourite cousin had visited.

He spoke of the destiny ring and of the seed, the tree and its curious fruit, of his wife and her spending spree, and of the treasure caravan that had transported him to the emperor's court.

Enrapt, Babur listened.

When his guest had ended his tale,
the emperor frowned.
'Might I ask who you are, then?'

Mustapha Khan sighed.
'I am a humble farmer with a lame donkey, a rocky field, a shack I built myself, and a most ferocious wife.'

The emperor drew breath.
'You are one more thing,' he said.
'And what is that, Your Majesty?'
'You are an honest man.'

The farmer felt his back warming with pride. A little unsure of what he was doing, he dug a hand into his pocket and clasped the crystal eye.

'Take me back to my own life,' he mumbled.

In the blink of an emerald eye,
Mustapha Khan was standing in his field.
But rather than being rocky and unkempt,
it was the very finest field, with the most
luxuriant crop of maize for a hundred
horizons. The lame donkey was gone,
replaced by a snow-white mare.

Anxiously, the farmer strolled past the mysterious tree grown from the seed in the ring, and up to the shack.

But the shack was no longer there.

In its place stood a lovely home, with a
screen of walnut trees at the front,
and flowers all around.

Before he had managed to step inside, Mustapha Khan was greeted with an embrace from the most lovely woman he had ever seen. Blinking, he realized it was none other than his own wife

That night, after a fabulous meal, the farmer climbed up to the roof and gazed at the stars.

First, he gave thanks for his adventure, then for being returned to his own life once again, albeit in a much-improved state.

After that, he thought of the destiny ring,
the tree and its seed, and of the crystal eye.

The eye.

Delving a hand into his pocket, he pulled it out and held it to the moonlight.
'Thank you, little eye,' he said.
The emerald eye seemed to blink, as though acknowledging the gratitude.

Then, warming on the palm of the farmer's
hand, it sparkled for a moment,
blinked a second time,
and vanished into the darkness.

Finis

About the Author

Descended from a long line of storytellers, writers, and savants, Tahir Shah is one of the most prolific authors of his generation. He has published more than sixty books in numerous genres, including travel, fiction, and fantasy, as well as tales for children.

Raised in the tradition of Eastern 'teaching stories', Shah is passionate about stories and storytelling. He regards the ability to learn from folklore as being in us all, what he calls a 'default setting of humankind'. As well as having written scores of books, Shah has made documentaries for National Geographic TV and The History Channel. He is the founder and CEO of the charity, The Scheherazade Foundation.

About the Artist

Esmeralda Riglea is an illustrator currently based in Romania. She studied art and illustration at university and has since developed her style using both traditional and modern techniques.

Esmeralda's main goal is to express her unique voice through the illustrations she creates, with inspiration drawn from music and personal experiences pictured in a metaphorical way..

Books By Tahir Shah

Travel

Trail of Feathers
Travels With Myself
Beyond the Devil's Teeth
In Search of King Solomon's Mines
House of the Tiger King
In Arabian Nights
The Caliph's House
Sorcerer's Apprentice
Journey Through Namibia

Novels

Jinn Hunter: Book One – The Prism
Jinn Hunter: Book Two – The Jinnslayer
Jinn Hunter: Book Three – The Perplexity
Hannibal Fogg and the Supreme Secret of Man
Hannibal Fogg and the Codex Cartographica
Casablanca Blues
Eye Spy
Godman
Paris Syndrome
Timbuctoo

Nasrudin

Travels With Nasrudin
The Misadventures of the Mystifying Nasrudin
The Peregrinations of the Perplexing Nasrudin
The Voyages and Vicissitudes of Nasrudin
Nasrudin in the Land of Fools

Teaching Stories

The Arabian Nights Adventures

Scorpion Soup

Tales Told to a Melon

The Afghan Notebook

The Caravanserai Stories

Ghoul Brothers

Hourglass

Imaginist

Jinn's Treasure

Jinnlore

Mellified Man

Skeleton Island

Wellspring

When the Sun Forgot to Rise

Outrunning the Reaper

The Cap of Invisibility

On Backgammon Time

The Wondrous Seed

The Paradise Tree

Mouse House

The Hoopoe's Flight

The Old Wind

A Treasury of Tales

Daydreams of an Octopus & Other Stories

Miscellaneous

The Reason to Write

Zigzag Think

Being Myself

Research

Cultural Research

The Middle East Bedside Book

Three Essays

Anthologies

The Anthologies

The Clockmaker's Box

The Tahir Shah Fiction Reader

The Tahir Shah Travel Reader

Edited by

Congress With a Crocodile

A Son of a Son, Volume I

A Son of a Son, Volume II

Screenplays

Casablanca Blues: The Screenplay

Timbuctoo: The Screenplay

A REQUEST

If you enjoyed this book, please review it on your favourite online retailer or review website.

Reviews are an author's best friend.

To stay in touch with Tahir Shah, and to hear about his upcoming releases before anyone else, please sign up for his mailing list:

 http://tahirshah.com/newsletter

And to follow him on social media, please go to any of the following links:

 http://www.twitter.com/humanstew

 @tahirshah999

 http://www.facebook.com/TahirShahAuthor

 http://www.youtube.com/user/tahirshah999

 http://www.pinterest.com/tahirshah

 https://www.goodreads.com/tahirshahauthor

http://www.tahirshah.com

www.ingramcontent.com/pod-product-compliance
Lightning Source LLC
Chambersburg PA
CBHW030520310726
48979CB00010B/1744/J
9781914960932